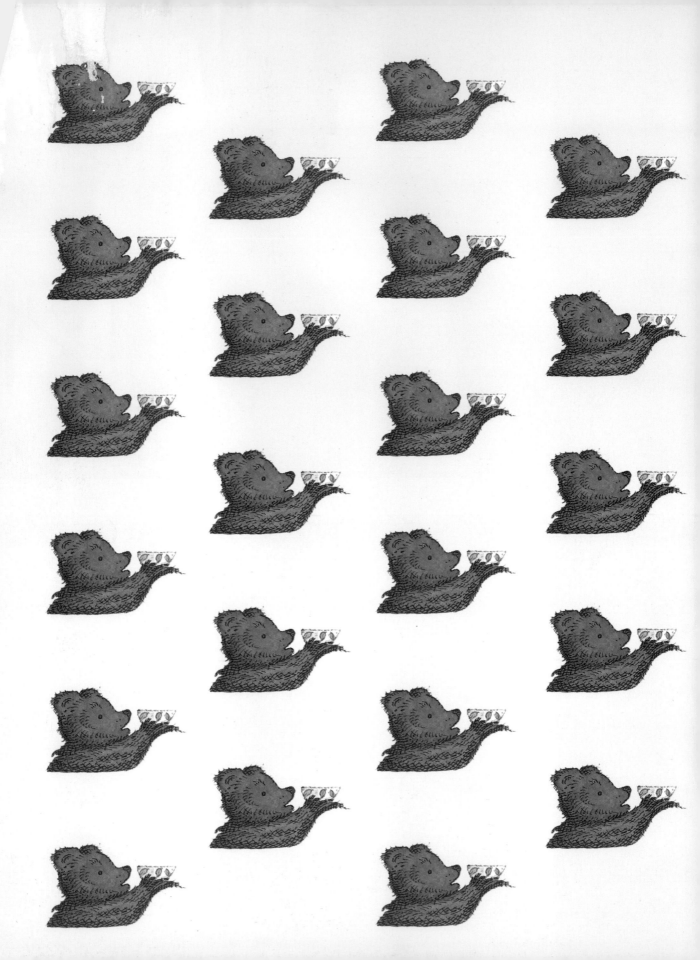

OXFORD
UNIVERSITY PRESS

Great Clarendon Street, Oxford OX2 6DP

Oxford University Press is a department of the University of Oxford.
It furthers the University's objective of excellence in research, scholarship,
and education by publishing worldwide in

Oxford New York
Auckland Bangkok Buenos Aires Cape Town Chennai
Dar es Salaam Delhi Hong Kong Istanbul Karachi Kolkata
Kuala Lumpur Madrid Melbourne Mexico City Mumbai Nairobi
São Paulo Shanghai Taipei Tokyo Toronto

Oxford is a registered trade mark of Oxford University Press
in the UK and in certain other countries

British Library Cataloguing in Publication Data available

ISBN 0-19-272-540-8

3 5 7 9 10 8 6 4

Typeset by Zoom Design

Printed in Malaysia

Goldilocks
and the
Three Bears

Ian Beck

OXFORD

UNIVERSITY PRESS

Once upon a time, and a long time ago, there was a little girl called Goldilocks. She lived in a house on the edge of a forest. Her father was a woodcutter, and every morning Goldilocks took his breakfast to where he was working. She liked to explore the forest paths, and one morning she found a path she had never seen before.

At the end of the path, Goldilocks came to a little house. She peeped in at the window and saw a cosy kitchen, with a merry kettle on the boil.

'I wonder who lives here?' she whispered to herself. 'It couldn't do any harm just to creep in and see.' So very quietly she lifted the latch and went in.

In the kitchen there was a shelf, with a row of honey jars; some big, some middle-sized, and some tiny. Whoever lives here likes honey, she thought. On the kitchen table

there

were

three

bowls.

Goldilocks said to herself, 'It couldn't do any harm just to have a little taste.' So she tried some porridge from the big bowl, but … *ouch* … that was too hot. She tried some porridge from the middle-sized bowl, but … *oh no* … that was too cold. She tried some porridge from the tiny bowl, and that was … *mmmmmm* … just right.

So she had another taste, and another, until the porridge was all gone. When she had finished the porridge, Goldilocks thought that she would like to sit down. There were three chairs.

She tried sitting on the big chair, but that was too soft. She tried the middle-sized chair, but that was too hard. So Goldilocks sat on the tiny chair, and that felt just right. But suddenly the chair fell into pieces, and she landed with a bump on the floor.

By now Goldilocks was feeling very tired.
Upstairs in the bedroom she found
there

were

three

beds.

She tried lying down on the big bed, but
that was too high. She tried the middle-sized
bed, but that was too bouncy. She tried the
tiny bed, and that felt just right. Goldilocks
yawned, snuggled up against the pillow, and
fell fast asleep.

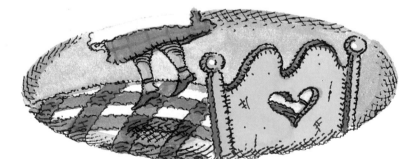

As Goldilocks fell asleep, the owners of the little house came back. They had been walking round and round the forest while their porridge cooled down. There were three of them. There was a daddy bear, who was very, very, big. There was a mummy bear, who was middle-sized. And there was a baby bear, who was tiny wee.

Daddy bear looked into his big bowl of porridge.

'Somebody has been eating my porridge.'

Mummy bear looked into her middle-sized bowl of porridge.

'Somebody has been eating my porridge.'

Baby bear held up his
tiny bowl.
'Somebody has been eating
my porridge, and it's all gone.'

Daddy bear sat down, plomp, in his big chair.

'Somebody has been
sitting in my chair.'

Mummy bear sat down in her middle-sized
chair.

'Somebody has been sitting in
my chair.'

Baby bear went to sit in his tiny chair,
only to fall,

bump,

on his bottom ...

The three bears made their
way up to the bedroom.
Daddy bear looked at his
big bed.

'Somebody has
been sleeping in my bed.'

Mummy bear looked at her middle-sized bed.
'Somebody has been
sleeping in my bed.'

Baby bear looked at his tiny bed.
'Somebody has been sleeping in
my bed – and she's still there!'

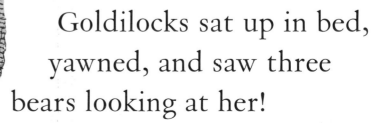

Goldilocks sat up in bed,
yawned, and saw three
bears looking at her!

'Little girl,' said daddy bear, 'did you eat our porridge?'

'Yes, I did,' said Goldilocks.

'And did you sit on our chairs?' said mummy bear.

'And break one?' said baby bear.

'Yes, I did,' whispered Goldilocks. 'I'm very sorry.'

'Well, never mind,' said mummy bear. 'You come downstairs with us, we've none of us had our porridge yet.'

Goldilocks sat on the middle-sized chair.

Baby bear said, 'You broke my chair.' So Goldilocks put the baby bear on her lap.

Mummy bear said, 'Whenever you want to have some porridge with us you are very welcome, but you should ask first.'

When Goldilocks said goodbye, she took the broken chair with her for her father to mend. After that she often visited the little house for porridge. And, of course, to play with baby bear.

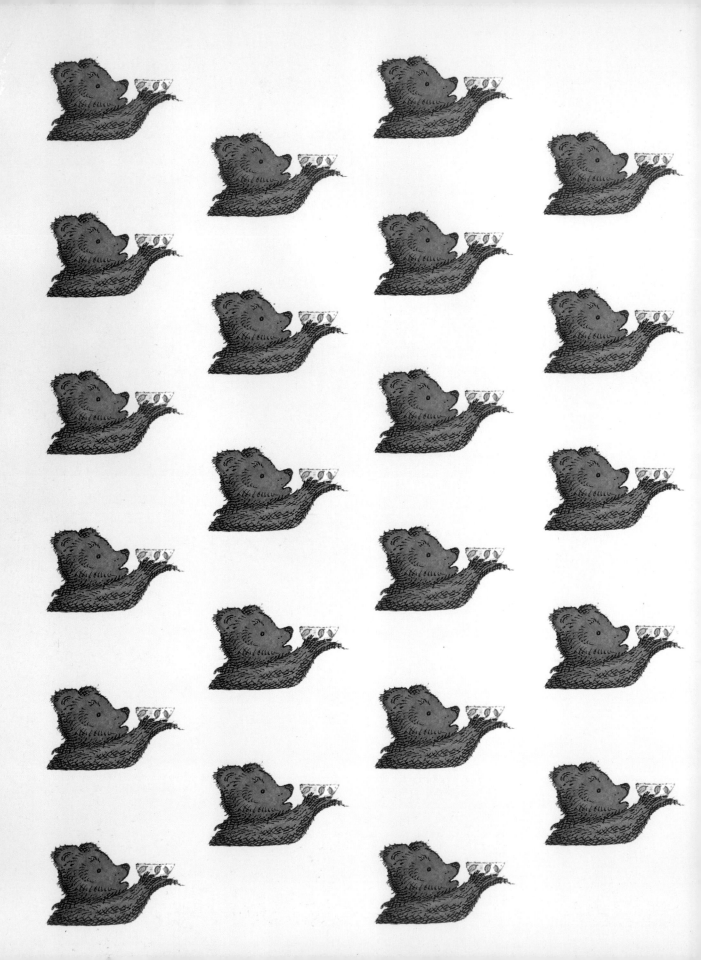